O Captain! My Captain!

*A Moving Elegy of Leadership, Loss
& National Mourning After Triumph*

A Modern Translation
Adapted for the Contemporary Reader

Walt Whitman

Translated by Tim Zengerink

Table of Contents

Preface Message to the Reader 1

Introduction 2

O Captain! My Captain! 8

Hush'd Be the Camps To-Day [May 4, 1865 9

This Dust Was Once the Man 10

Memories of President Lincoln 11

Thank You For Reading 24

Preface
Message to the Reader

Rebuilding the Greatest Library in Human History

Thousands of years ago, the Library of Alexandria was the heart of global knowledge — a sanctuary where the wisdom of every known civilization was gathered and shared freely.

And then, it was lost.

Now, we're rebuilding it — and you are invited to join us.

At the Library of Alexandria, we've set out to make every book available to every person on Earth — not just in print, but in every language, every format, and for every reader.

Here's how we do it:

- **Deluxe Print Editions at True Printing Cost** - Order any book as a high-quality paperback, elegant hardcover, or stunning boxset — and only pay what it costs to print. No markups. No middlemen.
- **Unlimited Access to the Greatest Works** - Enjoy thousands of timeless classics — from Plato to Shakespeare to Tolstoy — in beautiful, modern eBook and audiobook editions. Read and listen without limits — for every reader, everywhere.
- **Modern Translations for Every Language & Dialect** - We're reimagining the classics in clear, accessible language — and translating them into every dialect imaginable. Everyone deserves to understand humanity's greatest ideas.

When you visit **LibraryofAlexandria.com**, you're not just accessing books — you're joining a global movement to restore, preserve, and share the wisdom of civilization.

Join us today at LibraryofAlexandria.com

Together, we'll ensure the light of human wisdom never fades again.

With gratitude,

The Modern Library of Alexandria Team

Visit:
www.libraryofalexandria.com
Or scan the code below:

Introduction

The Paradox of a Nation's Triumph and Its Fallen Leader

Walt Whitman's *O Captain! My Captain!* endures not only as a poignant elegy to Abraham Lincoln, but also as one of the most emotionally resonant poems in American literature. Composed during a time of national upheaval and deep sorrow, the poem serves as a unique convergence of personal grief, political loss, and national identity. As a literary artifact, it stands apart from Whitman's typical free verse style—marked by its unusual adherence to formal meter and rhyme—and thus offers a strikingly structured expression of uncontainable emotion. For readers today, *O Captain! My Captain!* continues to serve as a lens into the American psyche at one of its most transformative and tragic junctures.

First published in 1865 shortly after President Lincoln's assassination, the poem immediately captured the public imagination. It was reprinted extensively in newspapers, anthologies, and schoolbooks, and became one of Whitman's most recognizable pieces—a distinction that often surprised the poet himself, who valued his more experimental work in *Leaves of Grass* above this mournful dirge. Still, Whitman understood its impact, and he came to embrace its significance as a national hymn of mourning.

This poem is more than a tribute to a president. It is an elegy to leadership itself—an expression of admiration, reverence, and personal identification with a figure whose moral clarity and steady hand guided a fractured nation through its darkest hours. It is also a lament for potential unfulfilled. Lincoln lived to see the end of the Civil War, but not the dawn of Reconstruction. He led the Union to triumph, but was denied the peace that he had strived to build. *O Captain! My Captain!* captures the ache of that cruel timing: victory tastes hollow when the victor is gone.

The poem is layered, complex, and achingly human. To read it is to enter into the heartbeat of a nation: relieved by victory, wrecked by loss, searching for a father figure in the wake of devastation. This introduction will explore the historical context of the poem, its structural and stylistic departure from Whitman's typical approach, and the broader emotional, political, and philosophical undercurrents that continue to make it a defining elegy of modern times. Through this lens, we hope to equip the reader with not just an understanding of the poem's content, but with the emotional and intellectual tools to feel its full depth.

A Personal and National Connection

To grasp the emotional intensity of *O Captain! My Captain!*, it is essential to understand the deep reverence Walt Whitman held for Abraham Lincoln. Though the two men never formally met, Whitman frequently saw Lincoln in person during his time in Washington, D.C., where he worked as a nurse and a clerk during the Civil War. The poet would often glimpse the president riding through the city on horseback or in a carriage. These sightings, though brief, made an indelible impression on Whitman, who came to view Lincoln as the living embodiment of the American ideal—both a symbol of unity and a man of profound inner strength and humility.

Whitman referred to Lincoln as "the greatest, best, most characteristic, artistic, moral personality of the century," and this affection was both political and deeply personal. He saw in Lincoln a kindred spirit—a figure of democratic virtue, plain speech, and deep compassion. When Lincoln was assassinated on April 14, 1865, just days after the Union victory, Whitman, like much of the country, was plunged into grief. Yet his mourning was not simply the mourning of a citizen for a leader. It was the mourning of a poet for a soul who had come to represent the very essence of America's struggle and potential.

O Captain! My Captain! was Whitman's immediate and visceral response to Lincoln's death. The poem's metaphorical framework—the ship's safe return to port, the fallen captain, the exulting yet grieving crew—provides a deeply resonant allegory for the Civil War and Lincoln's role in navigating the nation through it. The imagery is stark and symbolic: the "fearful trip" is the Civil War, the "ship" is the nation, the "Captain" is Lincoln, and the port is victory and peace. But the triumph is instantly shadowed by tragedy. The captain lies "fallen cold and dead" on the deck, even as bells ring and crowds cheer. It is this contrast—this wrenching juxtaposition of jubilation and sorrow—that gives the poem its enduring power.

Whitman's grief is structured but raw. Unlike most of his poems, which revel in open form, *O Captain! My Captain!* is tightly rhymed and rhythmically constrained. It reads like a dirge, a formal lamentation echoing funeral bells and muffled drums. Why this stylistic departure? Perhaps Whitman felt that the magnitude of Lincoln's death called for a ritualized poetic response, something accessible and ceremonious that could be absorbed by a mourning public. This poem is not just personal expression—it is communal ritual. It allows readers to mourn together, to honor a shared loss in unified cadence.

And yet, despite its accessibility, the poem contains layers of emotional nuance. The speaker is caught between the public celebration of victory and the private devastation of loss. The contrast is almost unbearable. The poem ends not with public triumph, but with the speaker retreating into solitude: "My Captain does not answer…/My father does not feel my arm…" The shift from "Captain" to "father" marks an emotional climax. This is not just a leader lost—it is a beloved paternal figure, a symbol of protection and wisdom, a steadying presence now gone. The reader is left on the deck, surrounded by flowers and flags, but empty in the chest.

It is this complexity of feeling—of celebration muted by grief, of love interrupted by death—that renders *O Captain! My Captain!* so deeply universal. It speaks not only to Americans mourning Lincoln, but to all who have ever felt the sting of loss in a moment that should have brought joy. It gives language to that particular kind of heartbreak, and in doing so, offers a shared place to lay our sorrow.

Mourning, Memory, and Leadership Beyond Lincoln

While *O Captain! My Captain!* was written in response to a specific historical moment, its themes reach far beyond the 19th century. The poem has become a universal elegy— adaptable to any context where leadership is lost in the moment of triumph, where nations or communities find themselves bereft of guiding voices, and where individuals seek to make sense of grief amidst celebration.

Perhaps the most famous modern revival of the poem occurred in the 1989 film *Dead Poets Society*, in which Robin Williams's character—an unconventional and inspirational English teacher—uses Whitman's lines as a metaphor for mentorship, rebellion, and the courage to lead a meaningful life. In this recontextualization, the "Captain" becomes not Lincoln, but a figure of moral courage and individual expression. This reinterpretation, though very different from Whitman's intent, speaks to the poem's enduring emotional truth: it is about what it means to love a leader, to depend on a figure who lifts us, and to feel suddenly adrift when they are gone.

In today's world—riddled with political fragmentation, social upheaval, and crises of trust in leadership—the poem resonates in new ways. It invites us to examine the kind of leadership we yearn for: moral clarity, humility, courage in the face of adversity. Lincoln, in Whitman's depiction, was not merely powerful; he was steadfast, sorrowful, and sacrificial. He bore the pain of the nation, and his death felt like a cosmic price paid for unity.

The poem also teaches us about the nature of collective grief. In our modern media-saturated landscape, we often struggle to find language that captures the scope of public sorrow. *O Captain! My Captain!* provides that language. Its imagery and rhythm offer a framework for ritual mourning—one that can be repurposed, revisited, and reimagined in response to contemporary loss.

At its core, the poem endures because it speaks to something deeply human: the desire to express gratitude, to name grief, and to reconcile joy with sorrow. It is a poem that gives us permission to feel two things at once—to celebrate a hard-won victory, and to collapse in tears for the one who didn't make it to the finish line. It is about the moments when the confetti falls, but the one we love is missing from the stage. About the parades we watch in silence because the one we wanted to cheer is no longer there.

As you begin your reading of *O Captain! My Captain!*, allow yourself to enter the poem with both historical understanding and emotional openness. See Lincoln through Whitman's eyes—not as a marble statue, but as a man who suffered, who persevered, who gave everything for a dream of unity. Read with your heart attuned to the complexity of grief, and let Whitman's words carry you to a place of both reverence and mourning. Let this poem be not only a tribute to a past president, but a meditation on what it means to lead, to follow, and to lose someone who once seemed irreplaceable.

In the end, Whitman does not offer consolation so much as presence. He stands on the deck with us, amid the garlands and the silence, and reminds us that to grieve is also to love, and to remember is to honor. The captain may be gone, but his voyage continues in us.

O Captain! My Captain!

O Captain! My Captain! our fearful trip is done,
   The ship has weather'd every rack, the prize we sought is won,
      The port is near, the bells I hear, the people all exulting,
      While follow eyes the steady keel, the vessel grim and daring;
         But O heart! heart! heart!
            O the bleeding drops of red,
               Where on the deck my Captain lies,
               Fallen cold and dead.

O Captain! My Captain! rise up and hear the bells;
   Rise up—for you the flag is flung—for you the bugle trills,
   For you bouquets and ribbon'd wreaths—for you the shores a-crowding,
   For you they call, the swaying mass, their eager faces turning;
      Here Captain! dear father!
         This arm beneath your head!
            It is some dream that on the deck,
               You've fallen cold and dead.

My Captain does not answer, his lips are pale and still,
   My father does not feel my arm, he has no pulse nor will,
   The ship is anchor'd safe and sound, its voyage closed and done,
      From fearful trip the victor ship comes in with object won;
         Exult O shores, and ring O bells!
            But I with mournful tread,
               Walk the deck my Captain lies,
               Fallen cold and dead.

Hush'd Be the Camps To-Day [May 4, 1865

Hush'd be the camps to-day,
  And soldiers let us drape our war-worn weapons,
  And each with musing soul retire to celebrate,
  Our dear commander's death.

No more for him life's stormy conflicts,
  Nor victory, nor defeat—no more time's dark events,
  Charging like ceaseless clouds across the sky.
  But sing poet in our name,

Sing of the love we bore him—because you, dweller in camps, know it
truly.

As they invault the coffin there,
  Sing—as they close the doors of earth upon him—one verse,
    For the heavy hearts of soldiers.

This Dust Was Once the Man

This dust was once the man,
  Gentle, plain, just and resolute, under whose cautious hand,
    Against the foulest crime in history known in any land or age,
    Was saved the Union of these States.

Memories of President Lincoln

When Lilacs Last in the Dooryard Bloom'd

1

When lilacs last in the dooryard bloom'd,
  And the great star early droop'd in the western sky in the
  night,
    I mourn'd, and yet shall mourn with ever-returning
    spring.

Ever-returning spring, trinity sure to me you bring,
  Lilac blooming perennial and drooping star in the west,
    And thought of him I love.

2

O powerful western fallen star!
  O shades of night—O moody, tearful night!
  O great star disappear'd—O the black murk that hides the
  star!
  O cruel hands that hold me powerless—O helpless soul
  of me!
  O harsh surrounding cloud that will not free my soul.

3

In the dooryard fronting an old farm-house near the white-
wash'd palings,
   Stands the lilac-bush tall-growing with heart-shaped leaves
   of rich green,
      With many a pointed blossom rising delicate, with the
      perfume strong I love,
      With every leaf a miracle—and from this bush in the
      dooryard,
      With delicate-color'd blossoms and heart-shaped leaves
      of rich green,
         A sprig with its flower I break.

4

In the swamp in secluded recesses,
   A shy and hidden bird is warbling a song.

Solitary the thrush,
   The hermit withdrawn to himself, avoiding the
   settlements,
      Sings by himself a song.

Song of the bleeding throat,
   Death's outlet song of life, (for well dear brother I know,
      If thou wast not granted to sing thou wouldst surely die.)

5

Over the breast of the spring, the land, amid cities,
  Amid lanes and through old woods, where lately the violets peep'd
    from the ground, spotting the gray debris,
Amid the grass in the fields each side of the lanes, passing the
    endless grass,
Passing the yellow-spear'd wheat, every grain from its shroud in the
    dark-brown fields uprisen,
Passing the apple-tree blows of white and pink in the orchards,
Carrying a corpse to where it shall rest in the grave,
  Night and day journeys a coffin.

6

Coffin that passes through lanes and streets,
  Through day and night with the great cloud darkening the land,
    With the pomp of the inloop'd flags with the cities draped in black,
    With the show of the States themselves as of crape-veil'd women standing,
    With processions long and winding and the flambeaus of the night,
    With the countless torches lit, with the silent sea of faces and the
      unbared heads,
    With the waiting depot, the arriving coffin, and the sombre faces,

With dirges through the night, with the thousand voices
rising strong
and solemn,
With all the mournful voices of the dirges pour'd around
the coffin,
The dim-lit churches and the shuddering organs—where
amid these
you journey,
With the tolling tolling bells' perpetual clang,
Here, coffin that slowly passes,
I give you my sprig of lilac.

7

(Nor for you, for one alone,
Blossoms and branches green to coffins all I bring,
For fresh as the morning, thus would I chant a song for
you O sane
and sacred death.

All over bouquets of roses,
O death, I cover you over with roses and early lilies,
But mostly and now the lilac that blooms the first,
Copious I break, I break the sprigs from the bushes,
With loaded arms I come, pouring for you,
For you and the coffins all of you O death.)

8

O western orb sailing the heaven,
Now I know what you must have meant as a month since
I walk'd,
As I walk'd in silence the transparent shadowy night,

As I saw you had something to tell as you bent to me
night after night,
As you droop'd from the sky low down as if to my side,
(while the
other stars all look'd on,)
As we wander'd together the solemn night, (for
something I know not
what kept me from sleep,)
As the night advanced, and I saw on the rim of the west
how full you
were of woe,
As I stood on the rising ground in the breeze in the cool
transparent night,
As I watch'd where you pass'd and was lost in the
netherward black
of the night,
As my soul in its trouble dissatisfied sank, as where you
sad orb,
Concluded, dropt in the night, and was gone.

9

Sing on there in the swamp,
O singer bashful and tender, I hear your notes, I hear your
call,
I hear, I come presently, I understand you,
But a moment I linger, for the lustrous star has detain'd
me,
The star my departing comrade holds and detains me.

10

O how shall I warble myself for the dead one there I loved?
  And how shall I deck my song for the large sweet soul that
  has gone?
  And what shall my perfume be for the grave of him I love?
    Sea-winds blown from east and west,
  Blown from the Eastern sea and blown from the Western
  sea, till
    there on the prairies meeting,
  These and with these and the breath of my chant,
  I'll perfume the grave of him I love.

11

O what shall I hang on the chamber walls?
  And what shall the pictures be that I hang on the walls,
    To adorn the burial-house of him I love?
    Pictures of growing spring and farms and homes,
  With the Fourth-month eve at sundown, and the gray
  smoke lucid and bright,
  With floods of the yellow gold of the gorgeous, indolent,
  sinking
    sun, burning, expanding the air,
  With the fresh sweet herbage under foot, and the pale
  green leaves
    of the trees prolific,
  In the distance the flowing glaze, the breast of the river,
  with a
    wind-dapple here and there,
  With ranging hills on the banks, with many a line against
  the sky,
    and shadows,

And the city at hand with dwellings so dense, and stacks
of chimneys,
And all the scenes of life and the workshops, and the
workmen
  homeward returning.

12

Lo, body and soul—this land,
  My own Manhattan with spires, and the sparkling and
  hurrying tides,
    and the ships,
  The varied and ample land, the South and the North in the
  light,
    Ohio's shores and flashing Missouri,
  And ever the far-spreading prairies cover'd with grass and
  corn.

Lo, the most excellent sun so calm and haughty,
The violet and purple morn with just-felt breezes,
The gentle soft-born measureless light,
The miracle spreading bathing all, the fulfill'd noon,
The coming eve delicious, the welcome night and the stars,
Over my cities shining all, enveloping man and land.

13

Sing on, sing on you gray-brown bird,
  Sing from the swamps, the recesses, pour your chant from
  the bushes,
    Limitless out of the dusk, out of the cedars and pines.

Sing on dearest brother, warble your reedy song,
    Loud human song, with voice of uttermost woe.
O liquid and free and tender!
O wild and loose to my soul—O wondrous singer!
You only I hear—yet the star holds me, (but will soon depart,)
    Yet the lilac with mastering odor holds me.

14

Now while I sat in the day and look'd forth,
    In the close of the day with its light and the fields of spring, and
        the farmers preparing their crops,
    In the large unconscious scenery of my land with its lakes and forests,
    In the heavenly aerial beauty, (after the perturb'd winds and the storms,)
    Under the arching heavens of the afternoon swift passing, and the
        voices of children and women,
The many-moving sea-tides, and I saw the ships how they sail'd,
    And the summer approaching with richness, and the fields all busy
        with labor,
    And the infinite separate houses, how they all went on, each with
        its meals and minutia of daily usages,
    And the streets how their throbbings throbb'd, and the cities pent—
        lo, then and there,

Falling upon them all and among them all, enveloping me
with the rest,
  Appear'd the cloud, appear'd the long black trail,
    And I knew death, its thought, and the sacred knowledge
    of death.

Then with the knowledge of death as walking one side of
me,
  And the thought of death close-walking the other side of
  me,
  And I in the middle as with companions, and as holding
  the hands of
    companions,
I fled forth to the hiding receiving night that talks not,
  Down to the shores of the water, the path by the swamp
  in the dimness,
    To the solemn shadowy cedars and ghostly pines so
    still.

And the singer so shy to the rest receiv'd me,
  The gray-brown bird I know receiv'd us comrades three,
    And he sang the carol of death, and a verse for him I
    love.

From deep secluded recesses,
From the fragrant cedars and the ghostly pines so still,
Came the carol of the bird.

And the charm of the carol rapt me,
  As I held as if by their hands my comrades in the night,
    And the voice of my spirit tallied the song of the bird.

Come lovely and soothing death,
  Undulate round the world, serenely arriving, arriving,
    In the day, in the night, to all, to each,
      Sooner or later delicate death.

Prais'd be the fathomless universe,
  For life and joy, and for objects and knowledge curious,
    And for love, sweet love—but praise! praise! praise!
      For the sure-enwinding arms of cool-enfolding death.

Dark mother always gliding near with soft feet,
  Have none chanted for thee a chant of fullest welcome?
    Then I chant it for thee, I glorify thee above all,
      I bring thee a song that when thou must indeed come,
      come unfalteringly.

Approach strong deliveress,
  When it is so, when thou hast taken them I joyously sing
  the dead,
    Lost in the loving floating ocean of thee,
      Laved in the flood of thy bliss O death.

From me to thee glad serenades,
  Dances for thee I propose saluting thee, adornments and
  feastings for thee,
    And the sights of the open landscape and the high-
    spread shy are fitting,
      And life and the fields, and the huge and thoughtful
      night.

The night in silence under many a star,
  The ocean shore and the husky whispering wave whose
  voice I know,
    And the soul turning to thee O vast and well-veil'd death,
    And the body gratefully nestling close to thee.

Over the tree-tops I float thee a song,
  Over the rising and sinking waves, over the myriad fields
  and the
    prairies wide,
  Over the dense-pack'd cities all and the teeming wharves
  and ways,
    I float this carol with joy, with joy to thee O death.

15

To the tally of my soul,
  Loud and strong kept up the gray-brown bird,
    With pure deliberate notes spreading filling the night.

Loud in the pines and cedars dim,
  Clear in the freshness moist and the swamp-perfume,
    And I with my comrades there in the night.

While my sight that was bound in my eyes unclosed,
  As to long panoramas of visions.

And I saw askant the armies,
  I saw as in noiseless dreams hundreds of battle-flags,
    Borne through the smoke of the battles and pierc'd with
    missiles I saw them,
And carried hither and yon through the smoke, and torn
and bloody,

And at last but a few shreds left on the staffs, (and all in silence,)
   And the staffs all splinter'd and broken.

I saw battle-corpses, myriads of them,
   And the white skeletons of young men, I saw them,
      I saw the debris and debris of all the slain soldiers of the war,
   But I saw they were not as was thought,
    They themselves were fully at rest, they suffer'd not,
   The living remain'd and suffer'd, the mother suffer'd,
     And the wife and the child and the musing comrade suffer'd,
     And the armies that remain'd suffer'd.

Passing the visions, passing the night,
Passing, unloosing the hold of my comrades' hands,
Passing the song of the hermit bird and the tallying song of my soul,
   Victorious song, death's outlet song, yet varying ever-altering song,
   As low and wailing, yet clear the notes, rising and falling, flooding the night,
     Sadly sinking and fainting, as warning and warning, and yet again
      bursting with joy,

16

Covering the earth and filling the spread of the heaven,
 As that powerful psalm in the night I heard from recesses,
  Passing, I leave thee lilac with heart-shaped leaves,
   I leave thee there in the door-yard, blooming, returning
   with spring.

I cease from my song for thee,
 From my gaze on thee in the west, fronting the west,
 communing with thee,
  O comrade lustrous with silver face in the night.

Yet each to keep and all, retrievements out of the night,
 The song, the wondrous chant of the gray-brown bird,
  And the tallying chant, the echo arous'd in my soul,
With the lustrous and drooping star with the countenance
full of woe,
With the holders holding my hand nearing the call of the
bird,
 Comrades mine and I in the midst, and their memory
 ever to keep, for the dead I loved so well,
For the sweetest, wisest soul of all my days and lands—
and this for his dear sake,
Lilac and star and bird twined with the chant of my soul,
There in the fragrant pines and the cedars dusk and dim.

THE END

Thank You For Reading

You've Just Read a Piece of the Greatest Library Ever Rebuilt

Thank you for reading.

This book is one of thousands we're restoring, reimagining, and translating as part of the **Modern Library of Alexandria** — a global movement to preserve and share humanity's most important ideas.

What was once lost to fire and time is now rising again — not just as memory, but as living, breathing knowledge, freely accessible to all.

What You Can Do Next:

- **Keep Reading.**

  Discover more legendary works — in beautiful print, audiobook, or digital form — at LibraryofAlexandria.com.

- **Build Your Own Library.**

  Every title is available as a paperback, hardcover, or collectible boxset — at true printing cost. Craft a personal library worthy of display.

- **Spread the Light.**

  Share this book. Tell others about the movement. Help us translate every timeless work into every language, so no reader is ever left behind.

By finishing this book, you've already taken part in something extraordinary.

Join us at LibraryofAlexandria.com

Together, we're rebuilding the greatest library the world has ever known.

With appreciation,

The Modern Library of Alexandria Team

Visit:
www.libraryofalexandria.com
Or scan the code below: